THE SCREECHING DOOR

THE SCREECHING DOOR

Three Spooky Tales

Jan Wahl

BearManor Fiction
2011

The Screeching Door: Three Spooky Tales

© 2011 Jan Wahl

For information, address:
BearManor Fiction
P. O. Box 71426
Albany, GA 31708

bearmanorfiction.com

Cover design by John Teehan
Typesetting and layout by John Teehan

Published in the USA by BearManor Fiction

ISBN—1-59393-370-3
978-1-59393-370-8

This is to Jonathan,
Alexander, and
Katherine Knoell

from Uncle Mouse

Table of Contents

THE SCREECHING DOOR

Or, WHAT HAPPENED AT
THE ELEPHANT HOTEL

for Jonathan

1

The Elephant Hotel

Great-winged, fluttering, white seagulls chased a flight of crows through the air. They wheeled low, screaming and yipping noisily. They hunted for something good to eat among the orange peels and banana skins that were on the surface of the water.

A big oil slick spread out over the water's surface. Ephram Effingham Runkle, Jr. thought it was a pretty crummy-looking seashore. So did his kid sister Myrtle Flossie. Not much of a place to spend the summer!

"*Yuuck!*" said both.

Disgusted, they rushed down the splintery creaky gray boardwalk that lay along the shore as quick as four legs could carry them.

Both shuddered at the idea of building dumb sand castles on the oily, gray-black sand. So

Ephram asked his parents, Mr. and Mrs. Runkle, who were lying in the middle of that sandy mess and liking it, "Hey! Can we leave this boring place and explore the village?"

"Ephram Junior!" sighed his mother. "Are you bored already?" She was wearing a tin-foil reflector and was greased with something like oleo. His father was wearing a Napoleon hat made of newspaper and a pencil was behind his ear.

"I suppose you can!" sighed Mr. Runkle. "PROVIDED you take Cicero along! Is it a deal?"

"It's a deal!" giggled Myrtle. Cicero was the decrepit family bulldog who could barely waddle. Anything to get out of there. Soon Cicero, dribbling saliva in the morning heat, was panting alongside Ephram and Myrtle like a rusty freight train.

At the end of the boardwalk stood an organ-grinder and his one-eyed monkey. The organ-grinder stopped grinding wheezy music and doffed a cap with a broken bird's feather on it. The monkey showed ugly teeth.

"Little boy! Little girl!" The organ-grinder grinned just like his partner, the monkey Chico. (The name was painted on the old green cup it was holding.) "You want *excellent advice*?"

"Sure!" said Ephram, wrinkling his nose.

The organ-grinder had warts and smelled like whiskey. He wiped his round yellow-pink nose on his dirty sleeve. He pulled his long moustache.

"First! A nickel for nice music! Eh?"

Myrtle fished into the pocket of her jeans and plunked in a nickel. "Shoot!"

The organ-grinder lowered his voice to a whisper. "Whatever you do — stay away from the Elephant Hotel! I'm not kidding!"

"Elephant Hotel?" cried both Ephram and Myrtle. "What the heck is that?"

But the organ-grinder shuffled off, nodding to himself. The monkey, Chico, turned around and craned its neck, gazing over its shoulder. It had a glass eye, but they noticed it was the wrong color.

The bright summer morning's sky was flooded with sunlight, yet suddenly they felt a strange chill in the air.

They hurried down Starfish Avenue into the village. Most of the houses had been built of wood at the end of the last century and badly needed paint. Gingerbread trim on the porches and under the eaves was rotting and falling off. Porches sagged.

Barefoot children played on weedy scrub-grass lawns. Old ladies and men rocked slowly on rocking chairs or swings, fanning themselves with palmetto fans.

Everybody watched Ephram and Myrtle as they went by. Brother and sister hurried on, turning down Seashell Road.

They passed the last of a row of tall, skinny houses. On the front steps perched a freckled boy practicing a tuba.

As they scurried by, he scowled, "FAT SUMMER CREEPS!" Then blew a loud raspberry on his battered, bent instrument.

Ephram glowered. The vacation was starting off kind of peculiar. Cicero panted and was no help at all, though he looked savage.

"Uhh, that your dog?" asked the tuba practicer.

"Sure is!" declared Myrtle. "He's a ten-time blood murderer. *He's got r-a-b-i-e-s!*" The saliva drooled out of Cicero's big mouth.

"Guess I take it back then," murmured the boy, struggling to push his wide tuba through the doorway.

"Phooey!" shouted Ephram, raising his fist, ready for a slug fest.

"Don't overdo it!" giggled Myrtle. They continued at a trot down the street. She patted Cicero.

"Summer folk aren't loved a whole lot," suggested Ephram. The bulldog had to pump his tired legs to keep up. "What a summer THIS is going to be!"

They crossed over to Wigglesworth's Ice Cream Igloo where the day's special was Pickled Pumpkin Delite.

TRIPLE WIGGLE
3
DIPS
99¢

The sign appeared one hundred years old.

The Igloo was leaning a little to one side. That didn't stop Ephram from ordering two Triple Wiggles for himself.

"Don't blow your whole wad, silly!" warned Myrtle.

Cicero stood nearby, eagerly waiting for ice cream to plop onto the sidewalk. A delicious half scoop slid down and obligingly plopped.

Brother and sister licked their cones as fast as they could. Ephram also bought himself a hefty supply of salt-water taffy, six Baby Ruths, and fifteen red licorice ropes.

"Can you tell us about the — um — Elephant Hotel?" he asked the Igloo lady. She became white as vanilla ice cream, let out a gurgling sound, and shook her head wildly.

"People around here don't mention it, kid!" she advised him. "Scram!"

So they did.

2

Tusk Message

Quickly they rushed down an alley, dragging themselves away from the sweet smells that came from the back door of Pomphret's Bakery, as they finished their cones. They approached a low, small, crumbly, purple brick dwelling. They couldn't believe it.

The cracked, broken sign said:

IZZY
  VALENTINE'S
    TREASURE
      ANTIQUE JUNQUE STUFF
    ROCK BOTTOM PRICES
  HUNT FOR YOURSELF

The tiny building was tucked into the alleyway, squeezed among garbage cans.

Suddenly, out from the store popped a grizzled-looking man wearing a tattered pirate's suit and a very dusty pirate hat, which he whipped off when he saw Ephram and Myrtle.

As he did this, a scrawny, moth-eaten parrot with most of its tail missing zipped out of the hat and circled the children. Finally it sat on its owner's bushy, orange hair.

The man was so tall you wondered how he fitted into the shop. "Allow me to present myself!" roared the proprietor. "I'm Izzy Valentine! On top of my head is my buddy, Captain Suchpowder!"

"Pleasedtermeetcher!" croaked the ancient green-yellow bird. Izzy Valentine clapped his pirate hat back on — on top of the bird, which continued talking. "Top of my... *buddy!*"

"Come in!" Mr. Valentine insisted. He stepped into the tiny place and made himself smaller by hunching over.

Tacked on the side walls were Victorian valentines with cupids shooting arrow, frilly ships, or boys and girls sitting on flower-bedecked swings.

"Come on! Don't be *shy!*"

In the middle of the clutter of outlandish objects, Ephram and Myrtle could see a huge, long-furred white cat flopped across a big mantel clock that had no hands.

"Meet Hepzibah the White Lady. Also my pal," cried their host. "Browse around!" So, since the children had nothing else to do, they moved into the shop.

It was loaded to the ceiling with bent bird cages, headless dolls, three-legged tables, a thousand horrible knickknacks. Even the children had to stoop over.

Hepzibah the White Lady yawned at them, flicking her feathery tail. A pink-winged butterfly or giant moth flitted into the shop. The cat jumped immediately into the air and gobbled it. Satisfied, she lay down again across the clock, shutting her furry eyes.

Ephram backed into a small yellowed clacking skeleton that hung in a corner. The bony hand fell, clapping him on the shoulder.

"*IIIICK!*" he screamed. Myrtle made a sound that was a half-laugh and half-burp.

"That's Miss Hortense, the World's Only Midget Opera Singer. She's only eighteen dollars!"

"No thanks!" decided Ephram, escaping through many dusty piles of junk.

Izzy Valentine looked disappointed. He asked, "Something cheaper?"

Myrtle, had not spent all her money on candy and was considering a pair of old brown snowshoes as well as some moose antlers.

Ephram flipped through a collection of hand-tinted postcards. The Chicago Fire of October 1871. The San Francisco Earthquake of April 1906. The Galveston, Texas, Flood of September 1900.

The sight of a miniature model of the White House made of pigs' teeth, inside a vinegar bottle, caught his eye. It was lying on top of a wobbly stand.

He scrambled toward it. In doing so, with one elbow he knocked loose an elephant's tusk that was nailed on the wall. Out fluttered a folded bit of yellowish paper which Myrtle caught. "Wow!" shouted Ephram.

Myrtle read the following:

> *Blueberry pie (ate 2)*
> *Veal dumplings (marvelous)*
> *Cherokee noodles (unusual)*
> *Macaroons (great)*
> *Fried parsnips (v. good)*

Apple fritters (chewy)
Raisin Cheesecake (fantastic)

"Is it a secret code?" asked Ephram.

Izzy Valentine grew wide-eyed. He stooped low to avoid hitting his head on anything, then rushed across the shop. He studied the piece of paper. At the bottom, he found in the tiniest of scrawls, "E.T."

"Elijah Tibbitt!" he whistled.

He looked scared.

"Who's that?" asked Myrtle, tugging at Izzy Valentine's elbow.

"The man murdered at the Elephant Hotel. Before I was born. This tusk is from the Elephant Hotel!"

The children moved closer.

"Mr. T.," Izzy whispered, "was a summer visitor. He was found one morning — with his neck broken. For years nobody returned there. EVERYWHERE — from Nantucket clear to Miami — they still say, 'Keep out of the Elephant Hotel!' It's boarded up. You can hear noises inside!"

Myrtle giggled. "A hotel for elephants sounds crazy."

"Where IS it?" questioned Ephram.

"Long ago," answered Izzy, "before this village had a curse, there was the *Snailshell* Hotel. The *Barrel* Hotel. The *Elephant* Hotel. Each was in one of those shapes. They were world-famous! Only the Elephant Hotel is left. It's never burned down, never been wrecked. Nobody here will go near it!"

"WHERE IS IT?" asked Ephram, insisting.

"One mile past the south end of the boardwalk. Outside of town," muttered the man in the pirate suit. "BUT KEEP AWAY!"

"Keep away! Keep away!" echoed a voice underneath his hat.

Myrtle bought the snowshoes for $1.87, and both children ran from the tiny shop.

3

Monkey Detective

Ephram and Myrtle hustled toward the boardwalk. Cicero panted from thirst. The sounds of swimmers splashing in the water ahead made the cranky bulldog pump his tired legs faster.

"What do you suppose that food list *means*?" asked Myrtle.

"I don't know!" answered Ephram. "It sure makes me *hungry!* What's there to do in this place, except EAT?" There was one thing: they could investigate the Elephant Hotel. How could they stay away from a place with a name like that?

They arrived at the boardwalk, and with a remarkable burst of speed Cicero trotted into the soothing water.

The children lingered by the hot dog stand counting the pennies they had left. Myrtle decided on a foot-long weenie and a raspberry fudge ripple cone. Ephram was placing his order when their father showed up in his Napoleon hat, glistening with sun tan oil. He looked sour-faced as usual.

"Why can't you kids act as though you're enjoying yourselves?" he begged. "Watch your mom out there!"

Mr. Runkle pointed to somebody in a green polka-dot swimming suit, paddling inside a gigantic inflated rubber duck. She grabbed the neck of it, kicking her feet in the water. She wore blue pontoon wings in case she fell off. "*Come on in!*" she yelled.

Mr. Runkle watched his children gobble their food. In a jolly tone he shouted, "I'll bet you'll be excited about *this*! Guess what's happening onshore tonight?"

Neither could guess.

Their father answered, "A terrific show, at nine o'clock! There's going to be a HORSE! With a LADY RIDER! Leaping off that far, tall tower — see it — EIGHTY FEET! STRAIGHT DOWN INTO DEEP WATER!

"WATER CLOWNS AND FIREWORKS, TOO! Bet you won't miss that!"

The children groaned.

It sounded corny to them — OK for grownups!

They were eager to explore the hotel.

So Ephram said: "Gee, Pop. We're awfully tired. You tell us how it was, *huh*?"

They left their father disappointed.

He walked toward the water's edge where his wife was drying herself with a towel. Cicero scrambled to meet him. Mr. Runkle turned, shaking his arm at them. Meaning: Stay away from the kitchen!

Back at the cottage (robin's-egg blue, Number 11), they plunged at once into the fridge.

They built sandwiches of salami, chicken, olives, onions, mustard, Swiss cheese, bologna, then added pretzels, corn chips, and walnut fudge and glasses of lemonade to go along.

They took the snacks to their rooms to wait.

They read till evening, which was balmy.

Their parents returned to change their wet clothes, and Ephram and Myrtle lay still, pretending to be asleep.

At last, the children really dozed — waking up now and again to hear handclapping from the crowd at the beach or the roar of clowns in funny motorboats or booming, crackling fireworks!

They heard their parents come home for the second time, whispering, preparing for bed, brushing their teeth, gargling.

They listened to old Cicero's wheezing slumber. They listened to the whine of mosquitoes and tough moths banging into screens. They heard the jiggly fan.

Finally, Ephram tapped the signal — three short taps — on the thin wall between their rooms. Myrtle tapped back. *Time to go!*

They sneaked out of the cottage. Myrtle held the kitchen flashlight. Ephram carried a hammer and crowbar.

Myrtle put on her snowshoes and walked on the soggy sand.

A three-quarter moon hung in the wide, starry sky that stretched above their heads.

Fireflies flashed by in the lazy night air. The shore was empty. The water was deserted except for a figure paddling a canoe through spooky starlight.

The water gently *slip-slap-slapped.*

The boardwalk ended.

Next, they walked for a mile or so through scrubby weeds, slippery stones, sticks, timothy, ferns, and wild oats. A land crab scuttled by, and Myrtle flopped over on the snowshoes.

"*Fizz* water!" she swore softly.

There was a rotting smell in the air — like vinegar.

Suddenly the giant hulk of an elephant, the center of the rotting odor, loomed before them.

"*YOW!*" the children bellowed at the top of their lungs.

The gruesome, ruined Elephant Hotel appeared as if it were lumbering across the sandy waste and had just stopped short.

On its back was a riding chair or basket, and on that stood the organ-grinder's monkey, waving a small flashlight at the figure in the canoe.

4

The Door Screeches

"Halt! Halt!" shouted the figure from the smoothly gliding canoe.

The craft was soon beached. The figure hurried up the shore. Chico the monkey gibbered hysterically, beaming the light at the children.

Myrtle switched her kitchen flashlight on him.

"Stool pigeon!" she hissed.

The animal's partner was, of course, the organ-grinder.

The man now introduced himself.

"I'm Detective Santuzzo." The monkey skittered down from the abandoned hotel and joined him. "That's private property!" he warned. "I get paid by our mayor to protect property! From vandals and busybodies. We don't want a new scandal or another murder! I told you, 'Stay away!'"

"Sir, we mean no harm," said Ephram

pleasantly. "If *you* were a kid and discovered the Elephant Hotel, wouldn't YOU be interested?"

Santuzzo scratched his grizzled head.

"By cracky, I guess I would, if I were a tot! Hey — but what about that crowbar and hammer?"

He looked at the two with suspicion. The one-eyed monkey jumped up and down, gleefully. "Why are you running around in the middle of the night?"

"Too hot to sleep," suggested Myrtle.

"Got to be prepared! In case we meet with weird customers!" Ephram added, trying to look small and not so fat.

"Yeah. Please let us *alone!*" announced Myrtle.

She gave her brother a push and they set out through the straggly weeds once more. They left the detective and the monkey jabbering together.

The children hid behind high ferns and watched the pair climb into the canoe and shove off, heading northward along the beach where the cottages lay.

"We've got to work fast," sighed Myrtle. "Perhaps he's going to wake Mom and Pop."

They returned to the shingled building, built exactly in the shape of an elephant.

There were boarded windows in each of the four thick legs and in the tin-plate stomach. The main door appeared to be located in the left rear leg. The riding basket was a roof garden.

Ephram took out his crowbar and started prying. When he got a board loose, splintery and gray, Myrtle's job was to knock it off with the hammer.

Rusty nails groaned. The boards made an X-shape across the door.

There was a horrible, sharp screeching — like some human cry.

The children, curious and dripping with sweat, cleared the pile of boards away. The door was locked!

They battered the bottom part through, leaving a hole. Ephram was too big to crawl through. So was Myrtle.

"You know what you have to do? Before anything else?" asked Ephram. "You are going to have to take off those dumb snowshoes!"

Myrtle, grumbling, unbuckled them.

Ephram jiggled the door handle. Then all of a sudden he turned stark white. Footsteps approached the door.

A *click* came on the other side.

"I think somebody's unlocking it!" said his sister.

The noise shuffled away, back up the left rear leg of the Elephant Hotel.

"Nuts!" cried Ephram. "I'm not spooked!" He tried the door, which this time opened .

The children entered.

Though it was hot outside, it was chilly and damp in the hotel. Half-rotted pine boards sank under their weight. Ephram readied the crowbar!

Rapidly Myrtle flashed the light up, down.

A framed, fraying piece of needlepoint read: WELCOME. As they went upstairs, they saw four alcoves set in the wall.

In the first stood a wood statue of Captain John Smith (waiting for Pocahontas). In the second was a short Abraham Lincoln (without hat). The third niche lay empty. In the fourth was General Custer (hanging about for a fight with Sioux Indians).

They seemed terribly real!

Ephram and Myrtle exited into the large stomach. Here was the registration desk and dining room.

Narrow ladder steps led up to the roof garden. Each of the other three legs, they found, was a little bedroom with simple furniture and a closet. The head of the elephant was the bath.

Everything was crammed together because of the building's shape.

Mouse tracks trailed across the buckled floor. Silky spiders' webs kissed their faces. Small as the Elephant Hotel was, while the children tramped through, they felt somebody *following*.

They could feel the structure shake as they stepped along. They heard sounds like somebody sighing.

"*Foood!*" a voice groaned.

The children remained still at least half a minute, making sure it wasn't THEMSELVES. The sighing continued.

"It must be a trick!" whispered Ephram. For the place was practically empty. Skimpy tables, chairs, curtains, but not much else. The hotel's kitchen and pantry were squeezed beneath the bath. Only a few soup spoons and meat forks hung upon the mildewed wall.

"FOOOOOD!" sighed the vague voice. Desperately.

"Er, speaking of food," said Myrtle. "Don't you think we could go home? To see what's in the fridge? I could eat a CAT!"

"So could IIIIIII!"

"WAS THAT YOU?" asked Myrtle sharply. Ephram shook his head. They rushed toward the exit.

Hustling down the left rear leg, they passed the alcoves. The flashlight's beam bounced along.

There were now four men standing in the alcoves — not three. Ephram whistled.

Beside General Custer and Captain Smith and Abe Lincoln stood a man in a long, old-fashioned nightshirt. He reached out to them.

The children tried to jump through the door together and got stuck.

"Get moving, Chubby!" yelled Ephram.

"Chubby yourself, Butterball!" yelled Myrtle.

Both pushed. Frantically.

They tumbled through — the sighing right behind them!

They collapsed outside in a rolling heap of waving arms and feet. They picked themselves up, and without bothering to glance back, hurtled along the weedy shore.

5

Olive-Grabber

Myrtle seized her snowshoes. The children darted into space. Sky, sand, water were a blur. They gasped for breath, arriving boggle-eyed in front of the Runkles' rented cottage, Number 11.

Their mother waited on the doorstep, drinking a chilled mug of root beer. She was making nervous lines in the sand with her bare toes. The children huffed and puffed.

"My babies!" she cried, rising.

"Um — hi Mom — how were the clowns? The fireworks?" asked Ephram, panting and looking over his shoulder.

"Where have you been?" she bawled. "*They're here!*" she called into the cottage. The lights were blazing. Their father was inside, working on office reports.

"What am I going to do about you kids?"

questioned Mrs. Runkle. "Maybe I'm a failure as a mother!"

The explorers rushed forward to hug and kiss her.

"Maybe we're failures as *children*!" Myrtle suggested.

"Look how FAT! Mom! How *FAT* WE ARE!" growled Ephram.

"Can't stop eating!" chimed Myrtle.

Mr. R. harrumphed nervously in the cottage.

"What would *my* mother have done, if I *sneaked out of bed and out of the house?*" Plainly Mrs. R. couldn't decide. She slipped away to get them root beers, since they were thirsty. Then she sat down again, starting to cry.

"If that wee monkey and the man with the moustache hadn't knocked at the door — we wouldn't even have KNOWN!" she blurted.

Could they tell her about the Elephant Hotel or the murder of Elijah Tibbitt?

Or those scary sighs?

Mrs. Runkle realized she wouldn't get a word out of them. She sat staring into the night.

Ephram and Myrtle were so angry at the stool pigeons, Santuzzo and Chico, that they stormed right past the refrigerator and headed for bed.

Their father was wearing a wet towel because of the heat. He glanced up from his stack of ledgers and papers.

"Well — came *home*, huh?" he volunteered.

They grunted.

"Listen. Tomorrow I'm going to rent a dune buggy. How about it? We'll have a swell picnic. How *about* it, Son? Myrtle?"

The children declared they would think about it. They shuffled off into their rooms and soon, like Cicero, they snored away into dreamland.

Their parents sat together on the cottage step and planned the picnic.

In the dazzling light of morning, which was bright as butter, all the Runkles were hungry.

Fried eggs and bacon disappeared in a twinkling, even though Mr. and Mrs. Runkle didn't eat half as much as Ephram and Myrtle.

After breakfast, Mr. Runkle fetched the dune buggy and bought two quarts of Wigglesworth ice cream. The buggy's color was tomato-orange.

Myrtle helped her mother prepare molasses baked ribs. Ephram's contribution was a towering heap of lobster-potato fluff. The bulldog wagged his tail.

They loaded the food and two striped umbrellas into the red-orange buggy. Mr. Runkle drove like a demon along the shore. "Go *south!*" urged Ephram.

Mr. Runkle steered in zigzag fashion, causing his wife to yowl. So did Cicero. The children grabbed onto picnic baskets to keep them from bouncing out. Cicero practically flew away!

"What the heck is that?" wondered their father, craning his neck, as they whizzed past the Elephant Hotel.

"Why don't we eat *next* to it?" offered Ephram.

Myrtle kept quiet and serious.

"Well! If we *do*, I'm not going to look!" exclaimed Mrs. Runkle determinedly. "Gives me the willies!"

Mr. Runkle, intrigued by the goofy ramshackle building, screeched the brakes, then backed up — bumping down the beach.

"Look, Ginger. There are shade ferns," he said, parking the buggy. Round, lazy, milkweed puffballs whirled through the afternoon sky. Ephram and Myrtle jumped out. Cicero barked crazily.

"*Shush!*" hissed Myrtle. Ephram laid out the checked tablecloth.

Their mother stepped down, pushing warily through blowing puffballs.

Mr. Runkle at once circled the hotel by foot.

He declared, "This thing has been boarded up *for years.*" The children gazed at him, astonished.

Sure enough, every board was nailed back on the door. The place seemed untouched!

Mrs. Runkle pulled down the vizor on her sun hat and refused to face the strange-shaped wreck.

She set out pickle jars in high fern grasses.

Out on the water, men in tiny, bobbing boats fished for mackerel and cod. Everywhere floated restless gulls. Myrtle and Ephram would have been bored by the picnic before it started, except for the fact that the hotel stood near.

Each Runkle brought out picnic containers. Soon, despite the heat, they were munching away.

Cicero dozed upon a moss patch under a sycamore. Suddenly Mrs. Runkle scolded, "WHO ATE EVERY SINGLE *OLIVE?*"

The children rolled their eyes innocently.

The olive container, at the edge of the fern grove, lay stark empty.

Mr. Runkle asked: "Do they *ever* tell the truth?"

Mrs. Runkle accused the children with a look.

"Didn't get ONE single olive. Cross my heart!" cried Myrtle, crossing it.

"Cross mine too!" seconded Ephram, quickly.

From deep in the ferns (but nothing was seen there) issued a burp.

Next a weird — extremely hungry — *sigh*!

6

A Chair Visitor

Hot and sleepy, the Runkle family climbed into the orange-red buggy. Cicero barked and snapped at the air though not even a dragonfly or hornet was beside him.

The other passengers stared ahead.

Suddenly Cicero stopped snapping, and sat contented, as if being tickled under his loose-hanging chin.

"Dumb dog!" scowled Ephram.

Cicero — or something — *sighed.*

Mr. Runkle drove back to the cottage. The children rushed to the Igloo for cool Lemon Fudge. The ice cream had melted.

It was too humid to walk to Izzy Valentine's shop. Yet there were many questions they hoped to ask about Elijah Tibbitt and the strange noises in the hotel.

When possible, they walked under shade trees.

They passed the tuba player — tootling "Polly Wolly Doodle." He was purple-faced from his effort in the blistering heat.

"Where's your dog?" the kid asked them halfheartedly.

"Careful! I'll *SIT* on you!" grunted Ephram.

That's all he had to do to win *any* fight.

The kid oom-pahed a march in the dizzying heat. It just wasn't worth it!

Brother and sister returned to the robin's-egg blue cottage with canary trim. Their parents were paddling out in the ocean, happily.

Myrtle, who had the key, unlocked the door. The cottage was a mess. "Cicero!"

Cicero seemed to have demolished two roast chickens for supper and left the bones on the floor. Yet he was tied up, whining and whimpering. The leash did not stretch to the refrigerator. The children were puzzled.

"How did he *do* it?" asked Ephram, scolding him while Myrtle swept up bones.

The dog stared in the direction of Ephram's room and whimpered. The boy ran to his room. A terrible snoring racket came from the direction of the bed! Ephram began to look for a horsefly.

When Mr. and Mrs. Runkle sloshed in from the beach, Myrtle and her brother were sitting casually, playing Parcheesi.

"Where's tonight's *chicken?*" cried Mrs. R.

The children rose together, glum-faced. They shook their heads.

Their father waggled a finger in anger: "There's one punishment — let 'em go to bed WITHOUT EATING!"

Ephram and Myrtle accepted this unfair fate without protest... what good would it do? They took their books to their beds.

They smelled luscious summer sausage. The horsefly seemed to have left. But Ephram had the eerie hunch he was not alone in his room.

The adult Runkles retired to bed early. From time to time Cicero moaned and howled at moonbeams.

Through the night Ephram listened to the tick-tick of his watch and a strange sighing. The same sighing he'd heard at the Elephant Hotel.

He stuck his head under his pillow, but couldn't get rid of the feeling that something was there in the room with him, sitting in the straight-backed chair.

Several times Ephram fell asleep. He'd awake, scratching mosquito bites, sitting smack up, staring into the darkness.

Keeping his eyes fixed on that chair.

The snoring was still there, and it was surely no horsefly. It must be an invisible person.

Elijah Tibbitt?

7

Haunted Breakfast

Knock! Knock! Knock!

It was Myrtle calling, "Breakfast! Are you there?"

Usually Ephram was the first out of bed, since then he had time to eat more. He stretched and gazed about his little room.

He half-remembered a dream in which he believed Elijah Tibbitt had been sitting in the chair at the foot of the bed.

The brilliant sun stung his eyes. He put on his bathing suit in a hurry.

His father insisted on giving Myrtle and him swimming lessons. Uggh! Ducking your head under water — somehow he'd get out of it!

Everybody in the family was in bathing suits.

Myrtle and Mr. Runkle were at the table already. Myrtle and Ephram's mother, bustling about and banging the lids of two pots together like cymbals, announced the menu:

"*Tomato juice! Soft-boiled eggs! And pecan huckleberry waffles! Coffee! Milk!*"

It was sort of skimpy, thought Ephram. But if you had had no supper the night before, it was good enough.

Mrs. Runkle got the eggs out.

"*One more egg,*" demanded an unseen voice.

Everybody glanced at Cicero drowsing in the corner. If it were Cicero, he startled himself. Half out of his bulldog mind, he skittered wildly away, clicking paws over linoleum in sheer panic.

"Who's the wise guy ventriloquist?" giggled Myrtle in bewilderment.

Just then, at the opposite end of the table, appeared a withered claw of a hand — nothing more — clutching an egg spoon.

The floating hand rapped the spoon sharply on the tabletop.

"ONE MORE *EGG!*" cried the voice, repeating the order.

"One more egg!" agreed Mrs. Runkle in an odd voice, and put five eggs into the bubbling, boiling water. She looked peculiarly nervous.

The voice had been a hand's voice so Myrtle handed him, or it, a glass of tomato juice, adding, "Worcestershire sauce, sir?"

"Please," answered the hand's voice.

At this point Mr. Runkle felt *he* should add something, so he queried, "Scorcher, yesterday, wasn't it?"

"Pardon?" impatiently asked the voice… the hand. Instead of small talk, it craved food. Ephram and Myrtle knew how it felt.

"Scorching weather. Hot!"

"You might declare so. However, this is a beautiful week to me. I just emerged because somebody for the first time opened my DOOR."

Myrtle and Ephram exchanged wise nods.

Mrs. R. bustled about spryly, clattering china, clanking pans, stirring waffle batter. Her theory was, if the hand were hungry, she ought to feed it.

Ephram set another place.

Five eggs came out of the water in two minutes. There were three kinds of toasted bread: rye, pumpernickel, raisin.

A second trembling, clawlike hand appeared to help the other butter toast and break the egg. These were swallowed into an invisible stomach.

"Forgive!" sighed the voice. "Until yesterday I had not eaten for eighty-four years! EIGHTY-FOUR! *I have quite an appetite.*"

Mrs. R. at once realized her children were innocent of the olive-chicken crimes. "My babies!"

The ghost kept eating noisily, wolfing down its food, demanding more all the time.

ALL the Runkles served it.

Canned salmon! Nutmeg pancakes! Tapioca! Lemons! Baked beans! Creamed onions! Rolled oats! Red beets! Cole slaw! Salami! Sponge cake! Mushroom soup! Sliced tongue! Apple pudding!

All vanishing in a twinkling.

"MORE!" the ghost shrieked.

Reluctantly, Mr. Runkle offered the thick, juicy porterhouse steaks for Saturday's dinner, while Myrtle made crunchy peanut butter-blackberry jam sandwiches, and Ephram dug out the Eskimo pies he'd hoarded in the freezer.

"M-O-R-E!"

Mrs. Runkle was making a pizza, and Ephram pulled out a hidden box of chocolate nut bars.

"Mister, this breakfast is costing a fortune! Have a heart!" begged Mr. R. — wishing he were back at his office. Mrs. R. wobbled dizzily.

Myrtle served a two-gallon batch of elderberry Kool Aid, then collapsed, exhausted.

By now the famished ghost began showing his parts.

The arms — the legs — the neck — the head.

He was dressed in nothing but a pale pinkish nightshirt. His skin was yellowish. Sunlight flickered right through his bones.

He introduced himself:

"I am Elijah Tibbitt who died alone and friendless — at the Elephant Hotel. I am a ghost, but I don't know WHY. I just remember I loved to eat. I guess that is why I came with *you*. You look like you like to eat!"

The ghost yawned. "If there is nothing more to eat, with your permission I will now take a nap!"

Then, already familiar with the house, the figure wandered away toward Ephram's bedroom and shut the door.

They heard the bedsprings squeak as the ghost settled down.

Mrs. R. was studying dirty dishes grimly.

Everybody pitched in silently, till Mr. R. spoke. "Ginger, what if Mr. Tibbitt follows us back home? *What if he follows us the rest of our LIVES?*"

8

Enchanted Band Aid

On the boardwalk a man with a round yellow-pink nose and long moustache sold balloons. A one-eyed monkey sold balloons also.

From cottage Number 11 stepped a bathing-suited family: father, mother, a fat boy, and a fat girl. They were accompanied by an old, skinny shadowy man and a bulldog.

The old fellow, dressed in a pale-pink nightshirt, carried an inner tube and wore enormous sunglasses.

"Hi there, Mr. Santuzzo!" called Myrtle. She waved at the shabby detective.

On behalf of the village, he was just about to accuse the children of breaking into the Elephant Hotel. It was he who had boarded up and locked the door.

However, his eyes witnessed a magic trick: a

43

pair of *sunglasses* and an *inner tube* moved through the sparkling air.

"I'll never touch whiskey AGAIN!" he promised. "YIIIIiiiii!"

Mr. Santuzzo ran down the boardwalk, letting go of balloons right and left. The monkey jabbered, following him. Both jumped into the frail canoe — paddling away, abandoning the detective business.

Mr. Runkle began to give a swimming lesson.

Because Elijah Tibbitt felt that a ghost ought to learn too, he joined the class. All those years he had heard people splashing outside so cheerfully! Myrtle and Ephram grew interested in the course.

First came the dog paddle.

Demonstrated by Cicero clumsily.

"If a dog can do it — *I* can!" declared Myrtle. If Myrtle could try it, so could Ephram, he announced.

Elijah Tibbitt took to water instantly. He showed them the Dead Man's Float.

The Side Stroke was next on Mr. Runkle's list.

Mr. T. flung aside his inner tube.

Merrily all three pupils attempted the Dolphin Kick (two truly gave a Whale Kick). Myrtle's favorite was the Australian Crawl.

Mr. and Mrs. Runkle watched their two children with tears in their eyes. Or was it from the salt spray? It was the first family occasion on which Ephram and Myrtle were not *grumbling*!

The children played tag around Mrs. Runkle's giant rubber duck, while Elijah Tibbitt clapped his hands with joy.

"I no longer feel I was cooped up *eighty-four years*!" he beamed. Hot sun shone straight through him.

He rolled and dived in and out, chasing Cicero. "YIPPEEE!"

By midafternoon the group was sprawled on the sand, telling jokes and eating hot dogs. Elijah Tibbitt flitted up and down the beach — drying himself off. Nobody else paid attention.

Was he invisible to everybody except the Runkles?

He executed a dance of Freedom — amazing for his age and condition. Next he told them why he had arrived at this summer village.

He had been lonely and longed to be among people. Nobody paid much attention to him then, either, even when he was visible!

"Wow," reflected Ephram.

"I know who might be able to see Mr. Tibbitt and maybe tell us why he's a ghost. Izzy Valentine!"

"Yep," agreed Myrtle.

Excusing themselves from their parents, they got dressed to march deep into the village. Mr. T. had nothing to wear but his nightshirt. Cicero trotted along.

On Starfish Avenue the barefoot ghost stepped on a broken glass sliver. He howled, leaping high in the air, and nearly fainted when he saw his pale-pink blood.

"Get him a Band Aid!" directed Myrtle. So her brother purchased one from Treech's Drugstore. Mr. Treech started wrapping the purchase.

"No — it's for our friend outside!"

Mr. Treech peeked out of the frosted store window. He glimpsed two children pasting a bandage onto the sidewalk. Or so it *seemed*. Then the Band Aid, the children, and a dog proceeded down the street.

"Mix me a double Sarsaparilla Punch," he told Hattie the soda jerk. "*Quick!*"

Elijah Tibbitt remarked to Myrtle and Ephram that there was not much change in the village.

Yet the instant he said this, the quartet passed the White Fox "E-Z" Laundromat.

He was fascinated. He drifted in and put his nose right up against the round porthole of a machine door, watching the clothes whirling in suds.

He could have watched that for hours. "*Laundromat! Laundromat!*" he tittered. Hearing the sound, glimpsing nobody, several ladies now scuttled away.

The children coaxed him to the street, meeting the surly, freckled tuba player — with groceries.

"Silly summer boobs!" he snarled. "Bet your CUR don't have rabies! Bet *YOU* do!" He gave a sharp, nasty laugh.

Myrtle whispered into Mr. T's ear.

The ghost shuffled.

The kid saw only a mysteriously flapping Band Aid circling around him.

"HOLYMOLY!" sputtered the boy. "I'm going NUTS! You must be *MAGICIANS!*"

Ephram and Myrtle bowed.

The tuba practicer high-tailed it in the opposite direction, seeking shelter at the firehouse — where the checkers players didn't believe him.

The children guided Mr. T. down the alley to Izzy Valentine's dingy establishment.

Izzy, in his pirate's suit and with Captain Suchpowder on his shoulder, popped out at the sound of customers. "Ha!"

In the darkness of the alley stood Elijah Tibbitt.

"You kids returning for my moose antlers?" asked the proprietor briskly.

Elijah Tibbitt, the Band-Aided, nightshirted ghost, gazed intently at Izzy Valentine (who did not see *him* at all), whooped, and fainted.

9

A Moon Clambake — Goodbye!

"Throw a bucket of water. Over there!" suggested Ephram. "*Fast!* Please!"

"On — WHAT?" thundered the bewildered proprietor.

"*You* can't see him. But he's there!" explained Myrtle urgently. "*ELIJAH TIBBITT!*"

To humor the kids, Izzy poured a cracked dishpan of water right where they pointed.

Fairly soon Mr. T. came around.

Ephram and Myrtle carried his body into the shop. Despite that nonstop breakfast, he was as light as feathers. They propped him up in a broken chair.

"*That man!*" groaned the ghost, as if choking. "*Owner of... ELEPHANT HOTEL!*"

Izzy lit a kerosene railroad lamp and scrutinized the chair seat. Magazines were piled high. On top of them was the mark of a ghostly fanny.

Izzy Valentine accepted this as proof that somebody was *sitting*. Hepzibah's white fur stood up as if electrified.

"Listen! I *confess*!" muttered Izzy numbly. "KEEP HIM AWAY!"

"Keep away!" echoed Captain Suchpowder, fluttering from wall to wall, and finally perching on a stuffed lizard.

Ephram demanded, "Confess *what*, Mr. Valentine?"

Izzy plunked himself down on a tippy stool next to the children. He grabbed a locked box from a nearby table.

"That *I* hold the deed to the haunted Elephant Hotel! However, Elijah Tibbitt is thinking of my grandfather, *Cadwallader* Valentine — the owner on the night of the murder. I look exactly LIKE HIM!"

With jittery fingers, Izzy pulled from his coat a photo of a man wearing an elephant trainer's costume. The ghost snatched it.

"My dad," Izzy went on, "and now me, hid in this back alley. In disguise. Because of the curse.

Once word spread OUR hotel was *haunted by the murdered gent*, whew!"

Izzy paused.

Unseen by him, Mr. T. was vigorously shaking the cobwebs out of his gray head.

"We boarded up the place. Ghosts usually stay where they die. But how I would have liked to carry on the hotel business!" Izzy declared.

Now Elijah Tibbitt trembled. "But I WASN'T murdered!" he cried.

He leaped from the chair, pacing around the junk strewn in the shop, remembering.

"I used to have a *worse* appetite than these two," he said. "I would draw up lists of favorite things. I would DREAM about appetizing foods! I would sleepwalk to raid the pantry!

"*That's what happened at the hotel.* I imagined I was back at my house — going downstairs to the pantry. Instead I plunged forward! BREAKING MY NECK!"

The elderly ghost sobbed — relieved to recall the truth.

Izzy grinned blissfully.

With the ghost gone from the building, the hotel might be restored. He'll sell antiques! Paint it white!

"*Break neck!*" said the parrot.

The children shook hands with Izzy, leading Mr. T. back to the boardwalk where they told the whole story to Mr. and Mrs. Runkle.

"LET'S HOLD A CLAMBAKE!" shouted Mr. Runkle after Myrtle, Ephram, himself, his wife, and Mr. Tibbitt had a celebration swim.

"YIPPPEEEEE!" bawled the latter.

"Invite *anybody* you wish!" roared Mr. R.

The Runkle parents and Mr. T. (who had been craving to visit a supermarket) bought ingredients. Myrtle trotted around to Izzy Valentine's shop. Izzy accepted merrily.

"Bring Captain Suchpowder and Hepzibah!" Myrtle directed.

Ephram went to invite the freckled tuba kid.

A frantic woman flew to the door with a mop in her hands.

"If you be summer folk — STEP AWAY!" she stammered. "We got *enough* trouble. With that hotel! I'm Mrs. Twigg — wife of the sheriff!"

"Who is it, Maw?" barked a voice. "Want any heads bashed in with the tuba?" The freckled boy glowered on the other side of the dented-in screen door.

"Inviting you to a clambake tonight! Take it or *leave* it!" grinned Ephram, simply. "I'm Ephram Runkle, Junior."

This invitation amazed the boy, who quickly replied, "Bartholomew Twigg. Call me Bumper. Geewillikins! A CLAMBAKE, Maw. I'll come if I can bring my tuba."

"Sure!" said Ephram.

Soon Bumper with tuba, Izzy in pirate's rig, Hepzibah led on leash, Captain Suchpowder jauntily on top of hat, Runkles, Cicero, and Mr. T. met in front of the cottage. "*Onward!*"

Carrying baskets of unshucked corn, salt, butter, potatoes, things for a clambake fire, they proceeded to a sand bar. A few babies with tin buckets and shovels stared at them as if this were an escaped circus.

Mrs. R., Myrtle, Mr. T. dug for clams.

Meanwhile, on the beach, Bumper, Izzy, Ephram, Mr. R. hollowed the pit, located stones, sticks, and dried seaweed.

"You only live *once!*" shouted Elijah Tibbitt, having a laughing fit.

When the fire was ready, and the stones were piping hot, they piled layers of corn, potatoes, clams, and seaweed down in the pit. Sweet steam sizzled.

During the clambake, Bumper was introduced to Mr. Tibbitt. Bumper glimpsed a (new) Band Aid, nothing else.

"*We've met!*" he roared.

Toward evening, Izzy performed the hornpipe, and Bumper was asked to toot on his tuba.

He played old songs which the ghost sang in a fine strong tenor. The best numbers were "Puttin' On the Ritz" and "Slap-Happy Joe." Izzy, Bumper, Hepzibah, and Captain Suchpowder excused themselves, wandering off.

"I used to be so lonely," whispered Mr. T. He looked closely at each Runkle. "Till I found *YOU!*"

Mrs. R. started wondering which room back home she could prepare for him?

Elijah Tibbitt gazed at them once more. The sun lowered in the vast sky. Already the moon was drifting.

That night the moon was not crescent-shaped and not round. It was exactly in the shape of a luminous soft-boiled egg.

Still, only Myrtle and Ephram (who saw Mr. T. best) and their parents caught sight of the ghost.

Slowly he walked away from them. The sky and water before him turned pink-purple. All at once he yanked off his nightshirt.

His withered shanks were an orange-peach color in the bright bright sunset.

The moon and sun faced each other. Water lapped. "He'll get CRAMPS!" cried Myrtle. "So soon after eating!"

"*No* he won't," promised Ephram, gently.

Fireflies flashed off and on like busy stars.

Elijah Tibbitt walked straight in, till the water reached his head. Breaking into the Australian Crawl, the old man swam steadily. Soon he was a speck *tipping over the far horizon.* Then, finally at rest, he vanished.

Ephram and Myrtle ran forward — to bring back at least his nightshirt. However, the sands turned faint pink. It was lost.

The Runkles sat watching the wide purple night and the slow egg-shaped moon. Then Mr. Runkle said, "Let's go home. Clambake's over."

Down the shore the Elephant Hotel seemed to sway and move in the dusk...

THE LITTLE TRAIN IN THE ZOO

Or, THE VERY PECULIAR TUNNEL

for Alexander

1

Introducing Nicholas and Trixie

Early on a summer's day, with black and gray clouds huddled off in a corner of the sky suggesting a possible rain shower, Mr. Greedle, a grumpy zoo attendant, unlocked the gates to the Humpty Dumpty Zoological Park.

"Hey! Just one danged minute!" he barked while he creaked the gates slowly on rusty hinges.

Mrs. Bump, the ticket seller, took off her patched white gloves and declared the Ticket Office open.

The parents rushed in with umbrellas, galoshes, rain hats, and children.

Straggly vines covered old metal fences surrounding the zoo. The popcorn man popped popcorn furiously. The cages had been swept pretty clean. The animals already had been fed their bran and dry vegetables and horsemeat and were waiting for visitors with bleary eyes.

The Lions, the Yellow Baboons, and the Brown Bears padded back and forth in their small cages, shaking sleep out of their fur, still half dreaming about where they came from — when earth and grass lay below their feet.

The Hyenas whined, and the Red Foxes panted. The Seals began their limbering-up exercises in and out of the water of the smelly pool.

The Crocodiles in the next pool yawned, showing great-toothed jaws. Children came and tossed peanut shells into Crocodile mouths and yelled and made silly faces. The Crocodiles did not seem to notice the peanuts were missing.

There stepped into the zoo park a brother and sister named Nicholas and Trixie — bored and anxious for something to do.

"What should we see first?" Nicholas yawned. "The Dromedary? Or the Anteater?"

"Sea Lions are best," claimed Trixie. "They're the funniest!"

The Sea Lions hit the ball with bellies, with flippers, and with heads, hard. They rolled underneath the water and then chased one another hysterically, wildly applauding themselves when they jumped above the surface.

Trixie laughed at them and they made foolish sounds. *Urrrk! Urrrk! Urrrk!* They danced in the air.

A keeper named Grimsbee came and tossed them some shiny small fish. "What an easy life they got!" he sneered. "Of course most everybody around here — everybody what ain't human, I mean — has only got to sit and get fed. Lazy, stupid things! *These* fellows jump for it, anyhow! Wish I had *me* a life that soft!"

Several minutes later, when Nicholas and Trixie departed to seek something more exciting, the Sea Lions watched their deserting audience and stopped applauding themselves with their flippers. They dived deep.

Meanwhile the sky grew darker, and faraway thunder rumbled, and the wetness was hanging high and pretty odd.

2

The Downpour

Nicholas and Trixie whizzed quickly by the
Night Apes and the Gorilla brothers, who reached
hairy arms out through the spaces between the bars
in front. Next by the Striped Hyena and Timber
Wolf and Coyote, all of whom circled their tiny
cages frantically, panting, hot-eyed.

Outside the Elephant House stood the giant
pachyderm Toots being scrubbed with a broom
by busy Grimsbee. Toots, who was old and got
tired easily, started to lie down, and while doing so
brushed against the keeper, who whacked her.

"You stupid beast! You could have *crushed* me!"
he yelled, getting red-faced, whacking again.

Nicholas kept thinking: *Suppose I was the one
who was locked up in the cage. How would I feel?*

Then the Tiger rolled over like a playful house
cat, and stretched, and licked his still-beautiful

furry coat, all the while keeping careful watch upon the boy.

Nicholas began trying to imagine where the cat had originally come from. As he stared, he began to see beyond the creature's cage. He seemed to see *dim blue mountains sitting in mist behind him. The lush green, shadowy trees in front. A sunny white, rolling river between, across which he might leap in one bound!*

The brother and sister passed the caged birds who could no longer fly and paused for a minute beside the Shoebills and the Spoonbills. The birds hissed and clucked and scolded.

Nicholas was trying to imagine them against a vast jungle sky, when a gigantic Jackdaw called out sharply. *"Oh, let us out of our cages!"* Nicholas anyway thought he heard the Jackdaw speaking, but Trixie poohpoohed it and yanked him away down the crunchy gravel path.

"Some Jackdaws HAVE been taught how to speak!" claimed Nicholas. And just as he said it, he thought he heard the strange black bird call out again, in a more pleading tone: "Let me, at least, out of *MY* cage!"

There was a growling up in the sky. A storm

was brewing. Perhaps it had been only the sound of thunder.

Suddenly thick rain, however, came pelting down. Nicholas and his sister dashed across the path and sought shelter in the Lion House.

In Which There Walk Three

The Strong smell of too many animals together in one place greeted Nicholas and Trixie. They joined a crushing crowd of parents and children waiting wetly in the Lion House, hiding from the buckets of hard pouring rain.

Three Chimpanzees, Toto, Curly, and Chipper, had been given the empty cage in the building because the Monkey House was overcrowded and a Spotted Leopard had recently died of the mumps. They were being forced by their keepers to put on a performance for the crowd.

The Chimps wore tattered clown hats and rode banged-up bicycles and swung absent-mindedly on grubby auto tires.

The great cats — the Jaguars, Panthers, Ocelots, the Puma, and the Cheetah — crouched in their corners glaring at the people. Lightning flashed.

Thunder grumbled.

The King of Beasts himself lay down lazily with his dull coat shedding and untidy.

"So *that's* the King of Beasts?" somebody in the crowd shouted. Everyone laughed. At once, the wheezing, mangy creature rolled over and roared majestically, and the crowd backed away quickly from his cage.

The great roar echoed throughout the building, and the other four-legged beasts immediately joined in, the echoes bouncing off the arched tiled walls.

All this time Nicholas couldn't help staring at the magnificent Siberian Tiger, who, whichever way he moved, managed to look Nicholas straight into the eye as if he expected to say something or would give a secret signal.

Suddenly the rain stopped. Sunlight poured into the building. The children and parents emptied it quickly with shouts of joy. Somebody had left a yellow rain slicker and hat behind, so Trixie picked them up.

"Let's go!" she urged. "Maybe we can find who they belong to!"

Nicholas glanced over his shoulder at the Siberian Tiger. It was like saying good-bye to a brother.

Trixie and he stepped down the wet gravel path which led from the building, and as they passed the Jackdaw's cage again, the Jackdaw said: "Listen, let me out. Be a sport!" Nicholas turned and observed that the padlock on the cage had not been completely snapped shut. Before he knew it, he found himself opening the door to the giant bird's cage. Trixie gasped.

"Quick! Put these on him!" he told her.

Together they helped the Jackdaw on with the rain slicker and hat for disguise. And then the three of them walked away.

4

The Journey Begins

"THANKS!" was the first thing the Jackdaw told them. "Thanks from the bottom of my heart. I promise you, you won't regret this!"

The second thing he told them was his name was Wilberforce.

He did resemble, pretty much, a small person snugly bundled up in the raincoat and hat, and nobody seemed to recognize that he wasn't, actually. Nicholas and Trixie introduced themselves, shuffling along past the tiny bleak yards that contained the Grévy's and Hartmann's Zebras.

There came from behind them tinkly music from the carousel plus the shrill hoots from the little zoo train.

"Hey — there's something I always wanted to do. Let's ride the carousel before we go!" shouted the disguised bird.

"Before we go where?" asked Trixie.

"Why," said Wilberforce, cocking his head sideways and looking at them intently, "for a ride on the zoo's train, of course."

The calliope jingled and jangled. The carved animals dashed around, around, around, bumping up and down. Nicholas had chosen an Antelope and Trixie a Dromedary. Wilberforce gripped the reins of his pink painted Hippo with his beak, growing giddy, obviously enjoying a very pleasant spinning sensation. When the trip was finished, the Jackdaw said again, with a queer glint in his eye: "What about riding the — um — TRAIN now?"

Trixie clapped her hands when Nicholas agreed.

The train's path threaded its way in and out of a tall long mound of grass-topped earth, and after this mountain it looped around half the zoo. The engineer was Mr. Ogg, a beet-faced, retired trainman who carried with him a tin flask containing rhubarb wine (made by his wife).

Numbers of parents stood by the railway's wooden railing, waving enthusiastically to their children who were settling themselves into the open cars. Three children fitted into each car, one child in front of the next. Some held bright balloons glistening under the sun.

"Hurry now — or we'll miss it!" shouted Wilberforce impatiently.

Nicholas, who had the cash, bought three yellow tickets, and they hustled to the end section of the train and climbed into the red caboose. Wilberforce sat in the very last seat of all.

Mr. Ogg, the engineer, sounded the whistle loudly and released the throttle. And off chugged the train! It started its journey past the Elephant House, where Toots, the ancient pachyderm, had now been chained fast by Grimsbee and was pacing crazily back and forth, swaying from side to side.

The little train moved faster past the crossing with blinking signal lights and then the soda pop stand and then the main zoo office and the aquarium. Now, with an extra burst of speed, it rolled straightaway into the pitch-black tunnel of the grass-covered mountain.

5

Switched Engineer

It kept being as black as a coal mine inside the tunnel, and the children began to squirm about in their rapidly moving cars, looking for the light at the end of the tunnel.

"Maybe — we should have waited for the next ride," suggested Trixie in a low voice.

"Why?" whispered Nicholas, thinking maybe it was an excellent idea.

"To have a chance to get a flashlight and bring some sandwiches," answered his practical sister from the seat behind.

"How could we guess it would stay dark for so long?" asked Nicholas.

The rattling train veered around invisible sharp bad curves. All at once they listened to the whooshing of wings — *slish, slap* — above them, moving faster than the train itself.

Trixie touched her hand upon the seat behind her… the last seat in the caboose. The Jackdaw had gone!

"That was *Wilberforce* you just heard flying away," she confided, leaning forward.

"Oh!" was the only thing Nicholas could mutter.

The little train swayed and lurched. Then they heard a horrible THUNK! — plus a groan — at the front end. A heavy object fell over to the side of the tracks.

"What was that?" inquired Nicholas a little nervously.

The train went sliding around a deeper bend, and only then for the first time could they glimpse a light ahead. A dim red glow at the end of the tunnel grew larger.

The train sped out fiercely from the darkness into a thick scarlet fog. Through the colored mist Nicholas and Trixie recognized that the figure at the throttle certainly was no longer Mr. Ogg.

It was Wilberforce, sitting there — dressed still in the getaway rain slicker and hat, steering them to they didn't know where. However they were sure they were *not* coming out at the zoo.

6

Pandemonium!

"WHERE ARE OUR CHILDREN?" the parents yelled as they waited and waited and waited.

The tracks running out of the mountain lay deserted and silent, and there was still no sign of the returning train or its small passengers.

There was a great hubbub while people called loudly into the gaping tunnel. Only the echoes of their own anxious voices returned: "Charlie!" "Hepzibah!" "Sam!" "Thelma!" "*Harold!*"

The chief of police had arrived, and he demanded a map of the tunnel.

"A *map* for a hundred-foot tunnel?" snorted Mr. Ephram Moodie, the president and manager of the Humpty Dumpty Zoological Park. Mr. Moodie was about to send forward a squad of handpicked men (including Mr. Greedle, the gateman, and Mr. Grimsbee, leading a mean-looking Police Dog named Fangbite on a chain) into the tunnel. They carried large flashlights and lanterns. As they were about to enter, out crawled, upon all fours, bumped and battered and black-eyed, the engineer himself, Mr. Ogg. Who said:

"I quit!"

A television camera zoomed up, and a man stuck a microphone in Mr. Ogg's face.

"*Something* attacked me," he wheezed. "Seized the throttle — that's *all* I know. Where the children *are* I couldn't *tell* you!" The zoo's special first-aid nurse, Miss Pynch, had to administer spirits of ammonia, but that is all they got out of Mr. Ogg.

Finally the day closed with a bright, full, silvery moon floating across the zoo park. Everybody wearily went home to sit by their telephones, convinced that the children no longer were on the grounds.

Mr. Greedle locked up the front, the side and the back gates, sticking the keys in his pocket, preparing to sit all night on watch.

The animals started chattering to each other — calling from cage to cage. The Panthers growled. The Lion and the Siberian Tiger shrieked. The Spider Monkey howled. The Falcons screeched.

The Red Foxes barked. They were excited and would not stop. Noises flew through the starry air.

"Hush up! Crazy critters! Go to sleep — or I'll turn the hose on you!" grumbled Mr. Greedle. While he wandered through the dewy grass to the place where he put his chair (DO NOT STEP ON THIS GRASS! the flaked-off painted sign commanded), he kicked the Peacock which was strutting directly in his way.

7

The Red Fog Lifts

While the train shot along, the red fog lifted somewhat.

"Listen, what is this? April Fool's Day?" asked one of the older children.

"No, it isn't," answered another tensely. "Be quiet!"

Chilly strong wind shook the ground beneath the tracks. The sky was now coppery and orange and gold. Nicholas watched the changing scenery with great curiosity. His parents had never driven here. The children could hear the eerie cooing of phantom faraway pigeons. Swarms of insects — locusts, katydids, crickets — also made sounds, and through the thinning-out reddish fog fireflies blinked on and off.

The train's passengers were carried into a marsh — where reeds and papyrus and odd plant life sprouted, where frogs croaked. Beyond the marsh grew clumps of lilies and forget-me-nots crowded and tangled together.

All at once, the train rushed alongside a great tall black Elephant standing in low, swampy water, lifting some weeds to his big high mouth with his trunk! About him, unafraid, waded a hundred white Pelicans at his feet.

None of the children dared say anything.

The train at that moment slowed down, because the tracks curved right around the edge of the water, and passengers wondered if the Elephant was going to charge at them. His tusks were long and gleaming and pearl-pink in the light.

However, he only gazed down at them with his tiny alert eyes and continued munching on weeds.

Soon the swamp turned into a river. There Water Shrews and Moles climbed up slippery banks and blinked at them with black-bead eyes. They scampered snuffling along. A Coatimundi (identified by Trixie from a photograph she had seen in a book) crawled along the muddy ridge, holding his barber's pole tail straight up.

"Where *are* we?" the children began to whimper, not accustomed to such sounds and scenery except on a television screen.

The train almost brushed against six shaggy-furred Water Buffalo with long, curved horns. The Water Buffalo drank from the purple velvety water, snorted, and raised their huge heads and studied the children just two or three feet away.

"WHERE ARE WE?" demanded one child now full of fear.

"There, there!" said Trixie, patting the child with one hand and reaching out her other to touch the nearest Buffalo's shaggy fur. Several other children leaned out to do the same, nearly losing their balance as the train chugged up a brief hill with a steep grade. At the same moment Wilberforce's raincoat dropped off.

There was a gasp from the children as soon as they realized their engineer was a Jackdaw. A hush like lightning fell.

At the top of the hill, the landscape changed quickly to a broad shimmering plateau upon which Zebras and Hartebeests and Antelope roamed freely knee-deep in grass. These animals were more muscled and bigger than the ones they had seen in the zoo. Beyond these grazing animals lay delicately-shaded mimosa bushes and the gigantic sinking sun, blood-orange.

The Antelope, the Hartebeests, the Zebras broke into a gallop in one big sunset herd. They aimed their hooves straight at the tracks! It made thunder on the ground. Dust flew beneath the animals' feet.

The children held their breath, most of them ducking down as the snorting, puffing beasts leaped, bounding over the train cars! The children could smell the animals. Not the smell of lazy, weakened animals in a drafty building — but the smell of activity and sweat.

Purple and violet and pink streaked the sky. Wolves and Jackals offered their mournful cries behind fig trees. The children shuddered.

The train was slowing. The Jackdaw let it glide through a grove of beautiful-smelling eucalyptus. Hanging Opossums blinked, wide-eyed, down at the passengers from every green-red low branch.

The moon, the same one that hung over the Humpty Dumpty Zoological Park, rose. But all the children were aware that it was like no other moon. It was much larger and nearer and made the kidnapped children solemn.

"All right!" cried Wilberforce, surprising them. He stopped the train and flew straight out of the front engineer's seat. "Here's where I get out. You drive it yourself! I'm home now, I'm *free!*"

He winked at Nicholas and Trixie. Then he flew off into the mammoth night sky, leaving them alone in an unknown landscape.

8

Monkey-Bread Trees

Many of the children stayed in their seats, mystified. More, however, scrambled out to stretch and mill around. The evening star stood out in the sky, followed by a thousand other equally bright stars. The children's stomachs rumbled, and they realized how late it was — how hungry they were!

"I really wish we'd brought egg and bacon and cheese sandwiches," complained Trixie.

"With *tomatoes!*" she added to herself dreamily.

A Black Stork and a White Stork lit from nowhere. Each stood on one long leg and examined the stranded passengers.

"Doesn't *anybody* know how to work this thing?" demanded Trixie from the rear of the train. This prompted Nicholas, who had once worked their model train, to march up to the front and tinker with the controls. Everybody got out while he tried. The train gave a violent jerk backward.

The two Storks seemed fascinated.

A huge cloud floated over the moon, and Nicholas continued to experiment in pitch darkness. When the moon came out again, Nicholas was splashed in moonlight so strong he had to squint his eyes. How tall the trees were! Songs of night birds were heard. The aurora borealis, or something like it, shimmered and flickered. It threw out every color of the rainbow across the sky.

Some of the younger children began to cry, "I'm hungry."

"Get it going!" Trixie urged her brother.

By now, by sheer lucky guesswork, Nicholas was handily managing both throttle and brake. So everybody jumped in. The train started. Not smoothly, but a start was a start!

They chugged up another steep grade — along through night-smelling groves and nighttime meadows. Out from prickly hedges there sidled, next to the tracks, Badgers and Weasels and Wildcats and Hedgehogs, gleaming-eyed, sniffing the strange scent. At last they approached an oasis of monkey-bread trees. Nicholas jammed on the brakes.

He turned around, addressing the passengers: "If it's good enough for monkeys, it's good enough for us, I guess!"

The children needed no further advice. They jumped out and shinnied up the trees and picked the ripest fruit, which was fine and did taste pretty much like bread. They shared it with each other and swung from branches like young monkeys.

With food in their stomachs they began to forget their fears.

It was Trixie, who had been acting as lookout from the top of the tallest tree, who mentioned that about fifty Lions were strolling toward them out of curiosity. They were male Lions, and their manes were not shabby like the one at the zoo but bushy-thick and vivid orange-yellow in the moonlight.

The Lions were not far from the other side of the train tracks when Trixie called out: "Let's hop back to the train! These Lions aren't hungry. We can't stay up here always. Let's just get in — slowly! If we don't panic, we're O.K."

"Right!" agreed Nicholas, who was the first to slip down from his tree. He sat back in the engineer's seat while the Lions walked right up to him. The other children followed his example gingerly and sat, stiff, waiting for the worst. The Lions stalked so close that their whiskers bent against the passengers.

The engineer started his engine. The Lions, startled, backed up — all fifty of them. The train roared forth, and the Lions imitated the sound and dashed after it playfully.

"Scat!" yelled Trixie from the caboose. "Go *home!*"

Which is exactly what a lot of the children were beginning to want to do.

9

In The Jungle

Although it was night, it was sticky and steamy. They passed a sign that read: JUNGLE.

Gigantic ferns and palm tree branches immediately arched above the moving train.

There were noises and silences mixed. Gibbering of Gibbons and Apes of all sizes, plus the racket from performing insects drummed into the passengers' ears. Toucans, Macaws, Parrots flew past the vines stretching overhead. Wasps buzzed along in the glowing velvety dampish dark. Lizards slid rapidly beside the train tracks, and Crocodiles gobbled Frogs. Cobras hissed softly. The children could smell cinnamon and pepper plants. Moths with large eyes painted on their wings blinked. Rich perfume from orchids caused everybody to grow dizzy.

Nicholas stopped the train beside a higher spot in the ground. Trixie and he put their heads together.

They decided to build wigwams out of palm leaves and bamboo sticks. The strongest among the boys broke off the bamboo. The air grew so hot that the children took their clothes off. After the wigwams for sleeping were finished, they found white empty anthills eleven feet high and slid down them since nobody felt quite sleepy enough yet.

A Leopard mother brought her cubs to watch this activity. And soon other animals gathered — Panthers, Pumas, and nine Cheetahs which were racing through. Wild Pigs stopped eating mushrooms and wandered very near. The children stroked the piglets' ears.

The passengers leaped and danced in the moonlight on the jungle grass. Bearded Monkeys joined them. The Leopard cubs purred, and Trixie gave one a noisy kiss. The cub licked her shoulder with a sandpaper tongue.

Finally the children were tired and went into the wigwams to rest.

A very tiny four-legged beast wandered into the girls' wigwam and began to sniff at Trixie's sweaty feet. Trixie stoked the queer beast. He had long fuzzy ears and a hairless tail rosy-pink and ratlike. He quivered for a minute, then settled down snugly in her arms, and they both fell asleep.

10

Three Signs

Sleep never came to Nicholas, and at first thin light of dawn he arose and stepped outside the boys' wigwam. What he thought he saw took his breath away. There in the mist were *dim blue mountains. The lush green, shadowy trees in front. A sunny white rolling river* between. . .

The eyes of the magnificent Siberian Tiger seemed to be staring at him again from somewhere, and Nicholas found himself thinking once again: *Suppose I was the one locked up in the cage. How would I feel?*

Now he whispered into the palm leaves to Trixie.

"Trixie!"

"What's up?" she replied, waking with a start.

"I've got a feeling that we must go back as soon as possible. Don't you?"

"Yep!" she replied, coming out with the queer beast in her arms. She put it on the ground. A bunch of Hummingbirds sailed down to hover around her hair.

"I'll have the train going in a jiffy," Nicholas said, putting on his clothes. Since Trixie was a born leader, she easily got the children up and led them to the train.

The Leopard mother lingered along the tracks. Trixie was wondering if she hoped to give a message to someone locked up at the zoo. The cat gazed at Trixie, then slunk away. Nicholas steered the train expertly out of the jungle while the children dressed themselves sitting in the cars.

They reached an area with stunted bushes and tufts of sparse grass. The bleached skeleton of what seemed to be a Wild Bull lay on white sand.

At this spot the tracks split into three routes. At the beginning of each stood a sign:

MOUNTAINS DESERT THE ZOO

"Which way do you want?" wondered the engineer. The children didn't even have to discuss it among themselves.

"*THE ZOO!*" shouted everybody. Thus Nicholas headed the train barreling down in that direction. They passed mango trees and cabbage fields and pine trees whose cones plopped onto their heads. The train chugged through a woods where Black Bears prowled and Spotted Lynxes and Moose and Elk wandered about.

Trixie kept watching from the caboose.

The blackest part of night was over, and dawn streamed over the horizon with a strange pinkish purple light.

A Rooster — someplace — started crowing.

A slight cool breeze fluttered lazy, drooping branches of a grove of willow trees. The tracks headed smack into them. The feathery branches tickled the children's faces. Before they knew it, they were entering the mouth of a tunnel.

11

Should They Telephone?

Mr. Greedle, perched on a weather-beaten kitchen chair, was fast asleep, snoring in a comfortable buzz, so he failed to hear the terrific clatter of the train ramming into the stout wooden post standing at the end of the line.

THONK!

Nicholas had laid on the brakes fully. At least so he imagined. But the wheels' pistons had not quite locked shut.

"Out!" declared Trixie, taking charge of matters. "Dust yourselves off, kids!"

It was a fact the passengers were dusty and thoroughly shaken. The front of the engine was crumpled a bit and the cow-catcher was mashed out of shape.

Every beast and bird inhabiting the Humpty Dumpty Zoological Park was wide awake, waiting up.

One of the children said, "Maybe we ought to phone our parents. Let them know we're all back!"

Trixie and Nicholas kept silent, but on the way they tiptoed past Mr. Greedle, who had the great chain of keys bulging out of his pocket.

Trixie stared hard at the keys and then at her brother. Nicholas, plus all the other children, began thinking the same thought.

So the telephone call was forgotten while Nicholas lifted the precious set of keys carefully, gingerly, quietly from the pocket while Mr. Greedle continued to snore.

It was early morning, and the other zoo employees would be arriving soon. The children would have to work fast!

Nicholas with Trixie's help scurried from cage to cage — clicking every padlock open. It took one complete hour to unlock every corner of the Humpty Dumpty Zoological Park. It was almost eight o'clock.

Each animal, each reptile, each fowl escaped into a new morning. Every child led or rode upon one creature, herding others forth. Hippopotamus! Reindeer! Marmoset! Elephant! Okapi! Ocelot! Penguin! Crocodile! Grizzly! Yak! Prairie Dog! *Everything!* Except the Giant Tortoise, Albert, who chose to remain where he was. Nothing could make him budge his shell from a tiny fenced-in concrete yard. He was too decrepit to care. He was one hundred years old!

Trixie and Nicholas were about to lead the procession, when the zoo keeper Grimsbee, having let himself in through a side gate with his keeper's key, leaped into their midst with his dog, Fangbite. Fangbite snapped and growled, showing yellow fangs.

"Just WHAT in heck's going on here?" Grimsbee bellowed — rubbing his eyes, trying to shake this amazing sight from his head. Greedle awoke, speedily rushing in also — brandishing his kitchen chair, screaming, "*Who stole my keys? Who stole my keys?*"

The animals, birds, and reptiles chafed and squirmed, ready to pounce on Grimsbee, Fangbite, and Greedle.

Instead, Nicholas, with the help of the Siberian Tiger, escorted the startled men into the cage in the Lion House, where the Chimpanzees, Chipper, Toto, and Curly, had put on their show.

"Hey! What do you think you're DOING?" barked Grimsbee.

"Listen! Ride those bicycles and swing upon those swings!" instructed Trixie.

Fangbite cowered in a corner of the chimps' cage.

The smaller animals, the birds, and the reptiles

got led into the cars of the train. The larger animals filed directly after them into the tunnel. Nicholas gave lessons on how to operate the train's engine to Chipper the Chimpanzee. The train started successfully, and the inhabitants of the zoo disappeared slowly into the tunnel.

The Siberian Tiger was the last to enter. He turned for a moment and stared deeply into Nicholas's eyes. The children waved goodbye, watching the creatures of nature go back to where they belonged.

A Jackdaw, black and glistening, sat on the front gate atop the sign that said *Humpty Dumpty Zoological Park.*

Then he lifted his wings and soared up into the beautiful morning sky, and the zoo was empty.

THE WITCH'S CLOCK

Or, THE CURSE OF THE WALNUTS

for Katherine

1

Hen Lottie

Her name: Lottie McPotty.

She was a witch. And wished to turn old Spook Owl into rice pudding just to scare him. She stared hard, truly hard — rubbing the red clock briskly. She said powerful words over it but got them mixed up. So by mistake had turned herself into a giant hen with blue spots. Quickly, Spook Owl swooped low and flew off to hide the clock.

Shouting, Lottie spun in a circle. "Can't make an excellent spell or undo this *without* my clock!"

She hunted everyplace. Down mouse holes. Under dry leaves. "Rats! Pumpkins! I'm lost without it!" And made fierce clucking sounds and plopped down beside a walnut tree, tapping ugly toes. "I've got to scare SOMEBODY!" She blinked round poultry eyes. The vision of a rabbit or squirrel jumping right out of its fur appealed to her.

At the top of the tallest tree in the woods the ancient owl sat watching.

"Ho. What's this?" wondered Lottie. Instead of rabbit or squirrel, a boy and girl trotted in her direction. They'd been sent to pick some wild walnuts. Their names: Sam and Rosa.

"Find me enough walnuts and I'll bake a cake," Ma had promised. They lived next to Deep Lake, a lake with no bottom. Pa lost his job in town so they moved into a sad tumbledown house. When Sam and Rosa left that morning, Pa was removing broken shingles from the roof.

Clouds passed across a sky that grew so dark the children stumbled in the path. Suddenly they heard *Tick tock! Tick tock! Tick tock!* A handsome red clock hung upon a limb of a gorse bush.

"No one must want that timepiece or they wouldn't hang it on a bush," reasoned Sam.

"We came for walnuts," said Rosa. She added, "Let's pick it anyhow."

On the other side of the bush Lottie kicked herself with a gnarly hen foot. If she'd only searched more she might have found it. However she only had a rather small hen brain.

Rosa removed the clock and as Sam and she

walked along she rubbed dirt and weeds away. The clock had a long cord which she wanted to hang about her neck. Sam couldn't help saying, "Wish *I* could wear it!" WHOOSH! It flew straight out of Rosa's hands.

"The red clock's gone!" she shouted.

"No. *Look*! I have it," said Sam. Then both of them knew it was special. It was magic.

"Well," said Rosa, "Let's test the darned thing." They happened to pause in front of the walnut tree behind which Lottie was hiding. "Let the baskets fill with walnuts," Rosa commanded.

Sam rubbed it again. A fierce storm of nuts thundered down upon them and soon they were knee-deep in walnuts. "Ow!" groaned Sam. The walnuts stung him and bopped him on the head.

"Hey! That's enough!" Rosa cried and now she rubbed the red clock; at once the walnut storm ceased. Both children stuffed the harvest into baskets and put more in their pockets. "This is enough for Ma's cake," Rosa said. "Let's go home."

The children stumbled on a tree-root sticking out across their path. The baskets tipped over, noisy nuts rolling out. Lottie the giant hen witch leaped forward, flapping ghastly chicken wings, screaming, "GIVE ME MY CLOCK!" She snatched it with sharp claws. Rosa and Sam hurled walnuts.

"*Enough! Quit!*" yelled Lottie McPotty.

For a split second the end of the cord dangled then into a hole in the ground. An opossum who happened to live down inside the hole instantly tugged at the cord — the red clock disappeared.

Lottie's eyes were angry marbles.

2

The Escape

"NOW you've done it," sputtered Lottie McPotty. "I'll turn you into grape sherbet!" Drumming her toes on the ground, she snapped with her huge beak furiously. Snip! Snap!

Quickly Rosa said, "Listen, if we get it back, will you let us go? Fix up our house — such a mess!" Lottie listened. These kids drove a hard bargain.

"The roof leaks!" Sam added. "A lot of walnut trees would be nice — Ma would like it."

Rosa chimed in bravely, "Pa can use a new truck."

The horrible hen batted eyes as big a golf balls. "Okay. *Just find the clock!*" She hopped closer and closer.

Down inside the hole the opossum picked up the clock and shook it vigorously; the ticking wouldn't stop. To tell the truth he preferred peace and quiet, that's why he lived in a hole. He tossed the clock back up.

"Remember your promise?" Sam asked.

"I *remember!*" shouted the spotted hen, eyes bulging with frustration.

"Then look behind you," he instructed her.

"If you're kidding, you'll be goners! I'll swallow you like worms!" Tilting her head, Lottie was delighted to discover the clock, which she swiftly picked up in her beak, putting the open loop over the tip of one wing. Rosa and her brother tiptoed away.

"*RRR-kkkk!*" snapped Lottie. "You leave without permission? Before I check to see if the clock is all right?" Rosa and Sam stopped in their tracks, knees wobbling.

She towered over them. "Wind the clock," Lottie demanded. "I can't do it with this idiot wing."

Sam wound it carefully.

"Remember your promise!" Rosa reminded her. The children were slowly backing away, hoping the hen didn't notice.

"Sure," clucked Lottie. Cooing softly, "I did *not* promise NOT to turn you into mice. For, say, five minutes!" Because out of the corner of her eye she spied Spook Owl, whose weakness was mice.

Against her feathered bosom she brushed the clock. Instantly Rosa and Sam were rodents.

"Run!" Sam squeaked.

"I'm running!" was Rosa's response. Away they went, however the great horned owl swooped down to snatch them, carrying them high in the sky.

"Listen, we're not mice!" squeaked Sam, but the bird paid no attention. "We're kids — all bones! No meat!"

"Cease wiggling," puffed Spook Owl — "I'm not as agile as I once was."

"That witch or whatever she is changed us," Rosa explained, yelling in his ear.

"Ah. That one," the owl hooted wistfully. "If I owned the clock! What wonderful things I would do! Amazing things..."

By then the five minutes were up. The children became normal size and were too heavy for the ancient bird. They slipped from his grip. "By gum — you're NOT mice!" he observed and down, down, down they plummeted.

"Flap arms!" Rosa instructed her brother.

"Doesn't help!" replied Sam. Down they went — by luck falling into Deep Lake. Home must be close by.

3

The Visitor

Despite the load of walnuts stuffed in pockets, Sam and Rosa swam quickly to shore, rushing toward a formerly tumbledown house flanked by an impressive grove of walnut trees. The witch did exactly what she promised.

"I guess a promise is a promise. Even if you are a witch!" Rosa decided.

"She's thrilled not to be a hen anymore," said Sam. Both children wondered how she looked now — would they recognize her?

Pa was calling. "Hurry! There are so many walnuts!" Ma brought out rakes and buckets. Ma and Pa were so busy they didn't ask questions. Anyhow the children knew the nuts ought to be picked before Lottie McPotty undid the spell.

Pa danced with joy; the unexpected walnuts will make them rich.

Ma was laughing — she hadn't done that in a long time. She had a plan. "I'll bake tons of cakes and we'll sell them!"

The family feverishly raked piles of walnuts until their hands bled. The round full moon came out. They realized it was hours past suppertime though they were too tired to be hungry… so they went inside to sleep.

"I don't remember a room with a polka dot door next to ours," yawned Rosa, "do you?" Sam felt just too weary to care.

Next morning they awakened to the enticing smell of cake fresh from the oven.

"Rise and shine, Sweeties," clucked a strangely familiar voice. "Your ma needs you to crack nuts. Your pa's already in town for supplies."

"Whose voice it it?" Rosa whispered to her brother. They peeked out: a plump figure in a polka dot dress went waddling away from their door down the hall to the kitchen.

"Wow," said Sam, "are you thinking what I'm thinking?" They dressed in a hurry to save Ma.

In the kitchen Ma was cheerfully singing. "Meet Mrs. Sparkle," she said. "The poor dear knocked at our door; she's got no home!"

The 'poor dear' was moving fallen cake crumbs around and around with a straw broom, pretending to do something useful. She tossed them a toothless smile.

Sam nudged his sister. "See that wattle hanging below her chin? Left over from being a giant chicken!"

Tall stacks of cakes lay everywhere. Then Pa appeared — driving a brand-new truck. Out he hopped, tipping his cap to the visitor, giving his wife a kiss, loading cakes onto the truck. The truck was pink with white polka dots.

Suddenly the woman with the broom spoke up. "Such lovely young-uns," she sighed. "Who sure can use a good scrubbing!" Ma agreed and went back to baking as Mrs. Sparkle pulled them into the bathroom. She filled the tub and dunked Rosa into it and almost scrubbed her hide off. "You are next, Cutie Pie," she informed Sam.

"No you don't!" Sam shouted. "You're a witch!" He zipped into the kitchen to warn his mother. "Ma, she's a witch!"

"Boo hoo!" blubbered Mrs. Sparkle, who abandoned Rosa in a sea of soapsuds. "You hear what he calls me?" And she retreated to the new room, slamming the door in a huff. More blubberish sounds flew out the keyhole.

Rosa dressed in a flash and shouted, "Ma, that's correct, she's a witch. Cross my heart!"

Ma was aghast. "Sam and Rosa," she declared in stern tones, "go to your room! Look how you made the lady cry!" They huddled in the hall and Rosa declared, "I bet she hopes to change us into something awful. Or worse."

Sam shuddered, next laid his ear tight against the door. Distinctly he heard *Tick tock. Tick tock. Tick tock. Tick tock.*

4

Deep Lake

Sam murmured, "The clock's close by — I know that crazy old witch has it."

"Well, she fooled Ma and Pa," said Rosa. "They're happy with a nice walnut cake business going! Swell roof and shiny truck!"

"Do you hear what I hear?" asked Sam. Down the chimney came a sound from the roof: HOO WOO. HOO WOO. HOO WOO. *The owl!* the children said in one breath. They weren't sure; was this a good owl or bad owl? Definitely it had an owlish appetite for mice.

The clock kept ticking at a fearsome rate.

Rosa decided, "That owl wants the clock — why don't we give it to him… he'll go away. He wants to make the woods a wonderful place, he says."

Her brother nodded. "I hope he'll turn her into something special, maybe a popsicle."

Rosa, examining blisters on her hands from raking, declared, "Don't want to see another walnut!"

"Me too," Sam agreed; his blisters hurt. The alarm on the clock went off and they heard a nasty voice.

"A reminder! I'm going to make two kids into grits and gravy!" This was immediately followed by a creepy chuckle. The children clutched each other.

Ma came down the hall. She wanted to know, "Aren't you ashamed you said what you said about Mrs. Sparkle? I'm waiting."

"Honestly, have you watched her eyes?" Rosa asked.

"Angry marbles," Sam said, nodding.

Suddenly puzzled, Ma leaned against the wall. She wondered, "Since when do we have a door with polka dots? Where did the trees come from? Have I been raking too much? I feel kind of dizzy."

All at once out in back came sounds of wild chopping. Ma and the children stared through the nearest window. A man helped Pa chop firewood — there were so many trees it was hard to breathe.

The visitor sprang out of her room. "That's my cousin Gooble Gobble," she explained. "A fine man." Ma looked at the visitor's eyes.

"Seems more like a troll," said Rosa. Her brother nodded. This was too much for Ma who raced into the children's room and plopped down on one of the beds, kicking her feet.

Mrs. Sparkle (or Lottie) followed her in. "That's right, little lady. Take it easy," she cooed. "Rest your bones! Me and Girlie will go crack walnuts!" Quickly she pushed Rosa into the kitchen.

Sam tried calming his mother. "Don't worry, Ma. Just stay there." And he went over to the polka dot door; it was locked. He tugged at Ma's skirt, steering her to the window. They both leaned out on the sill and Sam beckoned to the owl up on the roof.

Spook Owl flew down as Sam jumped out the window and then Sam discovered a small tub to stand on to reach the window of the witch's room. She liked fresh air so the sash was raised; the boy crawled in to sniff around.

Tick tock. Beneath one of the polka dot pillows lay the red clock. Sam called to the owl, leaped out and draped the clock's cord about the old owl's neck. The bird hooted gratefully and flew off.

Simultaneously came two commotions. One: Rosa was having trouble keeping the witch busy. "See? I can crack nuts with my teeth — you can't!"

Mrs. Sparkle's (or Lottie's) lack of teeth embarrassed her. "Another insult, Girlie! You'll regret it!" and she grabbed a rolling pin, chasing Rosa just as Ma appeared. Ma took a broom and swung it about with gusto. So the witch fled outside. Ma whacked the witch with all her might.

Two: Pa had become suspicious of the new hired man and said, "There's something funny going on! You look like a troll!"

"Funny, am I?" growled Gooble Gobble, who believed he was imitating a man quite cleverly. He swung his axe in Pa's direction. The two began to duel.

Axe blades gleamed in the noonday sunlight. Now, as the men dueled, the ladies did also, broom against rolling pin. This was the scene that met Rosa and Sam as they stepped into the backyard.

"Help Ma and Pa!" shouted the children and all at once, wearing the red clock, Spook Owl alighted and hooted, "Quick. *Rub the clock!*" So they did. The owl hooted a hoot heard even in the woods.

Whoosh! Bam! The witch and troll became fat mice.

Spook Owl carried them off holding one in each claw while both desperately nibbled at the cord that held the clock. The cord broke.

The owl tried as best he could, however mice and clock slipped away, falling to the bottomless bottom of Deep Lake.

5

What Then?

Sam and Rosa dashed over to the lake shore where Spook Owl circled, hooting frantically. The bird flew back to the children. Rosa's heart thumped until she realized the owl's eyes were friendly, in fact they twinkled.

Sam shook his head, saying, "Now you can't do the wonderful things you wished for. We're sorry."

"Lottie McPotty — that's the witch's name," the owl explained. "She plays tricks on those who live in the woods. I saw everything!" And he demonstrated how an owl can swivel its head in any direction. "I saw terrible things!" His feathers bristled.

The owl scratched his brow with one foot, remembering; then shut his eyes, thinking of the possibility of life without Lottie. He was at peace. The red clock lay lost at the unknown bottom of Deep Lake.

Ma and Pa invited the children and friend into the house; at first they were a bit wary, yet soon warmed up. Spook Owl promised to bring raccoons to pick walnuts. "They've got clever hands," he mumbled through a mouthful of cake.

Ma and Pa felt they might be dreaming. Helpful raccoons! Owls that talked! Witches! And trolls! Nevertheless Ma tied up fresh cakes for the owl to take home and Pa drove the old bird over to the woods in his splendid polka dot truck.

A pink sun was sinking beyond the blue lake and green woods and Rosa joined Sam, standing on the gray shore. All was calm.

One afternoon the children heard squeaking at the shoreline. They hid among long shadows of the trees. Two little mice in wet-suits scurried near, arguing quite animatedly.

"Won't do any good!" squeaked the first one. "If we find it, that clock will be chockfull of water!"

"Don't be stupid!" squeaked the second one. "A magic clock is forever!"

"If it doesn't work," replied the first one, "we are going to be *mice forever!*"

The other one fell silent. Then they began to argue again — until finally both little mice dived into the deep deep water, searching there excitedly. Chills jiggled up and down the children.

"Hey! Mice can't wind clocks, can they?" Sam blurted out.

"I hope not," shuddered Rosa. She didn't dare picture clumsy mouse paws winding the clock, causing monstrous mischief or mayhem.

Soon Rosa and Sam went into the house for a snack of Ma's tasty walnut cake. Serious raccoons busily tied purple strings. Boxes and boxes lay waiting for delivery. Ma's cakes had become the talk of the town.

Ma and Pa sat with the children while Sam shared once more the story of the red clock.

"Oh Pa," worried Rosa. "What if those mice find it before *we* do?" Neither Pa nor Ma had any answer to that.

Ma gave a little gasp. She liked being successful. A black gloom momentarily settled over the house — and the family huddled very very close.

It was just too awful to think about.

THE END

About the Author

JAN WAHL grew up in northwest Ohio and as a child played piano on a radio program called *The Kiddies Karnival*; also in grade school came the creation of traveling magic and puppet shows and shadowplays. Once he appeared onstage at the Toledo Town Hall Theater with the magician Harry Blackstone.

His more than 100 books for children have been illustrated by Uri Shulevitz, Norman Rockwell, Feodor Rojankovsky, Mercer Mayer, Steven Kellogg, Lillian Hoban, Cyndy Szekeres, Edward Artdizzone, Trina Schart Hyman, Edward Gorey, Peter Parnall, Mary Newall dePalma, Robin Jacques, Jeff Grove, William Joyce, Charles Mikolaycak, Fernando Krahn, Kay Chorao, Tim Bowers, Rosalinde Bonnet, Lee Lorenz, Leonard Everett Fisher, Michael McCurdy, Wendy Watson, Antonio Frasconi, Leonard Weisgard, Tomie di Paola, Fabricio Vandenbroeck, Monique Felix, Adrienne Adams, James Marshall, Blair Lent and Maurice Sendak.

He lives in Toledo, Ohio. His many awards now include the Avery Hopwood (for Fiction), Redbook, Ohioana and Parents Magazine as well as the Coretta Scott King and Bologna Youth Critics prizes.

www.ingramcontent.com/pod-product-compliance
Lightning Source LLC
Chambersburg PA
CBHW051839020726
47502CB00005B/1866